Private Joel and the Sewell Mountain Seder

This
PJ BOOK
belongs to

_____

_____

PJ Library®

JEWISH BEDTIME STORIES and SONGS

By **Bryna J. Fireside**

Illustrations by **Shawn Costello**

KAR-BEN
PUBLISHING

For Ella, Noah, Sophie, Ari, Lucy and Ximena—B.F.

Thanks to my family and friends and for
God's tender mercies and grace.—S.C.

CHAPTER ONE

Passover was just two weeks away. It was Private J.A. Joel's favorite holiday. But this year was different from all other years. It was 1862, and the Civil War was raging. Joel (called J.J. by his friends) was a Union soldier, fighting to defend his country and to free the Negro slaves.

Private Joel's company—the 23rd Regiment from Ohio—had spent months on an arduous march of several hundred miles through the West Virginia mountains, and had rousted the Confederate forces at Carnifax Ferry.

But all was pretty quiet now, and they were hunkered down for the winter in Fayette. Their assignment was to keep the railroad safe from attacks by Confederate soldiers who were hiding in the Sewell Mountains surrounding their camp.

If truth be told, the young soldiers were bored and homesick. And none more so than the 21 Jewish soldiers in J.J.'s regiment.

J.J. sat down with his closest buddies, Bill Leopold, George Lowenstein, Solly Richmire, and Isaac Ullman.

"Do you think Old Rosy will allow us to hold a seder?" he asked.

Old Rosy was their commander, William S. Rosecrans. The troops were very fond of him, though they never called him Old Rosy to his face.

"Well," said Bill, "Old Rosy is pretty fair."

"He'd understand how important this is," Solly chimed in. "I've never been away from home on Passover. In fact, this is the first time I've ever been away from my family. I sure miss them."

"Me too," said Bill. There was a moment of silence, as they each thought about their families back home.

They decided to compose a letter:

Dear Commander Rosecrans,

On behalf of the loyal Jewish soldiers of the 23rd Regiment, I request permission to observe the Jewish holiday of Passover, which begins at sundown on April 14th. This holiday celebrates the end of Egyptian slavery, when Moses led our people across the Red Sea to freedom.

Passover holds a special meaning this year. As soldiers, we are trying to defend our country and free the Negro slaves from their masters in the Confederacy.

We promise not to shirk our duties to the Regiment. But we ask your permission to prepare and hold a Passover seder, so we can recite the prayers and tell the story of how our people gained their freedom. We'd be honored if you would attend.

J.A. Joel

The very next day Old Rosy answered the soldiers.
"Yes, you may celebrate your holiday and have
leave to prepare for your special meal. I'd be
delighted to attend."

CHAPTER TWO

When word of the Passover seder got around, three Negro soldiers approached J.J. They were former slaves who had joined the 23rd Regiment.

"Private Joel," said Caleb Berger, "me and my buddies know something about your Hebrew Passover."

"How's that?" asked J.J.

"Well, when I was a young boy, I was sold to Master Berger. He was a Hebrew, and his family celebrated Passover. I worked in the main house and learned all the prayers. In fact, Master Berger taught me to read some English and Hebrew, and back in '59, when I was 16, he let me earn my freedom."

"Then how did you become a slave again?" asked J.J., full of curiosity.

"Well, I got caught in a round-up one night. It didn't matter that I was a free man. I got sold to one of the meanest masters ever to walk this Earth. That's where I met up with Abraham and Samuel. Soon after I was captured, I learned about the war to free us. But we didn't want to wait. We planned our escape and found the 23rd Regiment."

"And we would love to celebrate the holy day of freedom with you," Caleb finished.

"Would you help us prepare for the seder?"

"Yessiree," Caleb said. "Abraham and Samuel will help, too. Passover is for free men, and today we are free men."

J.J. looked at the three proud Negro soldiers. He felt a bond so powerful that it made him dizzy.

"It would be an honor to have your help," he said, "and to have you at our table."

CHAPTER THREE

The Jewish soldiers and the three Negro recruits met to figure out what they needed.

J.J. took charge. "First, we have to find a way to get matzah," he told them. "We'll have to pool our money to pay for it."

"That's easy," said Solly. "The paymaster was here just three days ago, and there's not much to spend our greenbacks on in this wilderness." All the guys chuckled.

"Just a minute, gentlemen," said a voice from outside the tent. "I, Greenberg, can help you."

Mr. Greenberg was not a soldier. He was a sutler, a man who traveled with the troops and sold them supplies such as shaving soap, razors, writing paper, stamps, and pens. And Mr. Greenberg was Jewish.

"I'm leaving for Cincinnati first thing tomorrow morning," he explained. "I will buy your matzah and send it back on the next supply train."

The soldiers each chipped in some dollars to give to Mr. Greenberg.

"Don't worry," he said. "I won't disappoint. Greeny always keeps his word."

Sure enough, in the wee hours of the morning of
April 14, the familiar clickity-clack got louder, as
the supply train drew closer to the village of
Fayette. It ground to a stop with a loud screech
and a puff of smoke. A cheer went up as the
soldiers began to unload the supplies.

"Look!" shouted Solly. "Seven barrels of
matzah–enough for the entire week of Passover!"

"And there's more!" exclaimed J.J. "Greeny sent
two Haggadahs and some prayer books!"

CHAPTER FOUR

Old Rosy gave the Jewish soldiers leave to get ready. Caleb, Abraham, and Samuel were given time off as well.

None of them had ever prepared for a seder. It was a job that had been left to their mothers, wives, or sisters.

But Caleb had helped his mama get ready for the Bergers' seder. "I'll be glad to help cook," he offered.

J.J. made a list of what needed to be done. "We don't have much time," he told them.

Seven men were assigned to build a log hut–a place to hold the seder. Abraham and Samuel volunteered to help them.

Four others hitched some horses to a wagon and rode off to the local farmers with a list of provisions for the traditional Passover meal of chicken soup and roasted lamb.

They also needed wine and the foods that go on the seder plate—an egg, parsley, charoset, and bitter herbs.

In the meantime, Caleb started the cooking fires and began heating large pots of water for

the soup. He gathered some metal rods, dug
a huge pit, and built a spit for the roast.

By mid-morning, the soldiers returned with
a lamb, seven chickens, dozens of eggs, and
bunches of carrots with green, feathery tops.

"We couldn't find any parsley," said Isaac.

"Or horseradish," said George, "but one farmer dug up something he said would be bitter enough."

He held up some long, skinny, green and red weeds that no one had ever seen before. Caleb washed away the dirt and chopped them up.

"Say," Bill asked, "does anybody know what part of the lamb goes on the seder plate?" No one knew.

"Well, if we roast the whole thing and put it on the table, we'll be sure to get the right part," Solly suggested. After much discussion, everyone agreed.

While Solly helped Caleb put the lamb on the spit, two soldiers chopped up the vegetables. Then Caleb set to cleaning the chickens for the soup.

Meanwhile, others were putting the finishing touches on the hut. J.J. directed the soldiers to set the tables for 26 men: 21 for the Jewish soldiers, three for the Negro soldiers, and one for Commander Rosecrans.

"Who is the extra setting for?" asked Samuel.

"In our family, we always set an extra place for the stranger," said J.J.

In the distance, J.J. saw George pushing a barrel up the hill. "You found wine?" he asked.

"No wine," said George. "Cider. It's been sitting around all winter, so it should be just right by now."

CHAPTER FIVE

"Hey, Isaac," called Solly. "The water is beginning to boil. We'd better get started with the matzah balls."

Isaac took some sheets of matzah, put them in a bowl, and beat them into fine crumbs with a hammer. "This looks to be enough," he said, when the bowl was full.

"Now what?" asked Solly.

"I think you put in eggs and water," Isaac offered.

Solly cracked a dozen eggs into the bowl, and Isaac stirred it all up.

They dipped their hands in cold water so the matzah mixture wouldn't stick. Solly scooped up some batter and rolled it around in his hands. "OK?" he asked, showing Isaac a rather lopsided ball.

"It's got to be more round," said Isaac. He took another handful of batter and rolled it round and smooth. "Pack it hard like a snowball," he said.

JJ. came to the cooking area. "I need the stuff for the seder plate."

"Ain't got no parsley," said Caleb, "but these carrot tops will do. They're nice and green."

"What are we going to use for the charoset?" asked JJ. "We don't have nuts, and we don't have any apples."

"Well," Caleb said, scratching his head. "That charoset—isn't it supposed to represent the mortar used for the bricks?"

"That's exactly right. Got any good ideas?"

Caleb reached down and picked up a brick from the fireplace. "Will this do?"

JJ. laughed. "Sure will. We can't eat it, but it serves the purpose. Let's see: We've turned cider into wine. We've turned carrot tops into parsley. We've turned this weed into horseradish. And now we've turned a brick into a brick!"

"Even if we don't get things exactly right, I'm sure the good Lord will accept our efforts.

"You know, fellows, this is going to be the best
Passover ever!"

CHAPTER SIX

It was nearing sundown, almost time to begin the seder. The Jewish soldiers, along with Caleb, Abraham, and Samuel rushed off to change into their dress uniforms.

When they arrived at the hut, they could not believe their eyes. The table was covered with a festive, snow-white cloth. There were candles, a plate of matzah covered with a colored napkin, and a huge round pan that served as the seder plate.

In the center of the plate was the whole roasted lamb, surrounded by a roasted egg, bitter herbs, the green carrot tops, and the brick. There were big jugs of apple cider. Next to each plate was a "wine" cup, and there was an extra cup for Elijah the Prophet.

"By golly, we've done it!" said Solly. "This is the real thing."

CHAPTER SEVEN

Outside in the soft spring breeze, the trees swayed, making gentle, rustling music. The glorious moon shone its full face into the hut. Everyone kept an eye on the sky and patiently waited for the first stars to appear, signaling the start of the holiday.

When J.J. stood up, a hush fell over the gathering. He welcomed everyone and thanked Commander Rosecrans for granting them leave to celebrate this festival of freedom.

A great cheer went up from the men as the soldiers applauded their hard work. This night was certainly different from all other nights and from all other seders.

Isaac lit the candles with the proper prayer. J.J. held up his cup of cider and recited the prayer for wine. "We're giving thanks for fruit of the vine, even though we're drinking fruit of the trees," he explained. "I think God will understand."

He followed with the traditional blessing of thanks:

"Blessed art thou, Lord our God, who has kept us alive, sustained us, and enabled us to reach this time."

Everyone drank the first cup of cider.

"Wow!" said Solly. "This packs a punch."

J.J. told everyone to take some carrot tops and dip them into the salt water. "We do this to welcome the spring, and to remember the tears of slavery," he explained.

Then he held up the matzah and spoke about the meaning of the "bread of affliction."

"This matzah recalls not just the suffering of the Hebrew people, but all people who have ever been slaves."

Caleb shouted, "Amen! May we all be free
men in America."

"Here, here!" the soldiers agreed. And in
the blink of an eye, they downed another cup
of cider.

"Slow down, fellows," J.J. said. "It's not time for the second cup, yet."

Those who remembered them sang the Four Questions, and J.J. continued with the Passover story. Out of the corner of his eye, he spotted three men sneaking an extra cup of cider.

Then everyone recited the plagues God sent down to punish the Egyptians. As each plague was named, the soldiers spilled drops of cider onto their plates. There was a rousing, if wobbly, rendition of the song "Dayenu."

J.J. explained all the items on the seder plate and passed around pieces of matzah. "It's time to put some of the bitter herb on the matzah and taste it," he said.

The soldiers were pretty hungry by then, so instead of taking just a tiny bit of the strange weed, everyone put a heaping mound on some matzah and gobbled it down.

What a mistake! When the herb touched the

inside of their mouths, tears sprang to the
soldiers' eyes. As they swallowed, they gasped
and clutched their throats. They reached for
the cider jugs, drinking cup after cup to quench
the fire.

Suddenly three soldiers jumped up. One shook his finger at J.J. "I am Pharaoh!" he yelled. "And I will never let your geeple po. I mean your steeple mo. Um, your people go."

Another shouted, "I am Moses and I am leading my purple, er my pupils, er, no, my people out of here."

"Don't worry, Moses, I'm your brother Aaron," said the third man, "and I'll help you escape from this Pharaoh. We'll see you all in the Promised Land." At that, the three men swooned.

So their buddies carried Moses, Aaron, and Pharaoh off to bed, while Caleb led the rest of the soldiers in singing the old spiritual, "Let My People Go."

CHAPTER EIGHT

Finally, it was time to eat. The soup was served. Each golden bowl had a perfectly round matzah ball in it.

"This looks interesting," said Old Rosy, who had never seen a matzah ball before. When he tried to cut into it, his spoon bent in half, but the matzah ball stayed smooth and round. He tried two more times.

"Well, men," Old Rosy said, "I see you Hebrews have invented a new weapon. If we can't eat this thing, perhaps we can shoot it with a slingshot."

"The matzah ball attack plan!" shouted J.J. And the soldiers applauded Solly and Bill.

After the last morsels of lamb were eaten, and
the last cup of cider sipped, the men sang all the
songs they knew until deep into the night.

And they prayed that with God's blessing, there

would soon be freedom for all those who were
slaves in America.

It was, J.J. recalled many years later, a Passover
seder no one would ever forget.

Author's Note

Many years ago, an article by Rabbi David Geffen in the Binghamton, NY *Jewish Reporter* captured my imagination. It was about a group of Jewish soldiers in the 23rd Ohio Regiment who celebrated Passover during the Civil War. Further research uncovered an article by J.A. Joel, "Passover–A Reminiscence of the War" which appeared in *The Jewish Messenger* April 1866, over 100 years ago. It gives many details about the seder which took place in the mountains of West Virginia. Surfing the web, I found the names of four more of the twenty-one Jewish soldiers who served in J.A.'s regiment: William Leopold, George Lowenstein, Solomon Richmire and Isaac Ullman.

I tried to imagine the seder and what these soldiers were feeling as they celebrated a holiday of freedom during the war that was being fought to abolish slavery in America . As my story took shape, I knew that I wanted to include some former slaves to share in this celebration. Over 180,000 African Americans (then called Negroes) served in the Union Army. Some served in all-Negro units commanded by white officers. Although Caleb, Abraham, and Samuel are the product of my own creation, there were former slaves who enlisted with whatever Union armies were nearby.

American Jews and African Americans have a proud history of fighting for freedom and civil rights in America and elsewhere in the world. As we sit down to our family seders, it is good to remember that in many parts of our world, there are still places where people are not free. –*Bryna J. Fireside*

Kar-Ben Publishing, Inc.
A division of Lerner Publishing Group
241 First Avenue North
Minneapolis, MN 55401 U.S.A.
1-800-4KARBEN

Website address: www.karben.com

Library of Congress Cataloging-in-Publication Data

Fireside, Bryna J.
  Private Joel and the Sewell Mountain seder / by Bryna J. Fireside ; illustrated by
Shawn Costello.
      p. cm.
  Includes bibliographical references
  Summary: A group of Jewish soldiers, and three freed slaves, have a Passover
seder in 1862 on the battlefields of the Civil War.
  ISBN-13: 978-0-8225-7240-4 (lib. bdg. : alk. paper) [1. Passover—Fiction. 2.
Seder—Fiction. 3. Jews—United States—Fiction. 4. United States—History—Civil
War, 1861-1865—Fiction.] I. Costello, Shawn, ill. II. Title.
  PZ7.F498719Pr 2008
  [Fic]—dc22   2007005275

Manufactured in the United States of America
1 – CG – 12/29/13

03145K1